THE NURSERY CAR
and
THE BiG RED TRAiN

HONK, BEEP, HONK, HONK, BEEP!
LITTLE BO PEEP HAS LOST HER SHEEP!
DRIVING THROUGH THE COUNTRYSIDE,
SHE SPOTS THE SHEEP, WHO JUMPS INSIDE!

Licensed exclusively to Top That Publishing Ltd
Tide Mill Way, Woodbridge, Suffolk, IP12 1AP, UK
www.topthatpublishing.com
Copyright © 2014 Tide Mill Media
All rights reserved
2 4 6 8 9 7 5 3 1
Manufactured in China

Written by Oakley Graham
Illustrated by Steve Richards

ISBN 978-1-78244-784-9

A catalogue record for this book is available from the British Library

Beep! Beep!

HONK, BEEP, HONK, HONK, BEEP!
THE OWL AND THE PUSSYCAT RENTED A JEEP!
NO LONGER AT SEA, ON THE BEACH THEY RIDE,
WATCHING THE STARS WITH AN EYE ON THE TIDE.

BEEP! BEEP!

HONK, BEEP, HONK, HONK, BEEP!
LITTLE BOY BLUE HAS FALLEN ASLEEP!
THE SHEEP AND COWS ARE RUNNING AROUND,
BUT THE WEARY DRIVER DOESN'T HEAR A SOUND.

HONK, BEEP, HONK, HONK, BEEP!
HUMPTY DUMPTY FELL OUT IN A HEAP!
ALL THE KING'S MEN TO THE RESCUE CAME,
NOW HUMPTY WILL NEVER DRIVE BADLY AGAIN!

HONK, BEEP, HONK, HONK, BEEP!
Wee Willie Winkie checks children are asleep!
Riding through town, in his blue nightgown,
His little old car makes the only sound.

CLICK, CLICKETY-CLACK, CLICKETY-CLACK,
THE BIG RED TRAIN RUNS DOWN THE TRACK.
PULLING OUT OF THE STATION WE'RE HOMEWARD BOUND,
WITH A CLICKETY-CLACKETY BIG TRAIN SOUND.

CLICK, CLICKETY-CLACK, CLICKETY-CLACK,
THE BIG RED TRAIN RUNS DOWN THE TRACK.
SPEEDING UP HILLS AND ACROSS MUDDY FIELDS,
WITH A CLICKETY-CLACK OF ITS FAST-TURNING WHEELS.

CLICK, CLICKETY-CLACK, CLICKETY-CLACK,
THE BIG RED TRAIN RUNS DOWN THE TRACK.
RACING ACROSS THE GREY CITY SCENE,
ITS WHEELS GO CLICKETY-CLACKETY-SCRRREAM!

WOO, WOOO!

CLICK, CLICKETY-CLACK, CLICKETY-CLACK,
THE BIG RED TRAIN RUNS DOWN THE TRACK.
TRAVELLING BESIDE THE SUNSHINY BEACH,
ITS WHEELS GO CLICKETY-CLACKETY-SCRRREACH!

CLICK, CLICKETY-CLACK, CLICKETY-CLACK,
THE BIG RED TRAIN RUNS DOWN THE TRACK.
THE JOURNEY'S OVER, TURN THE TRAIN AROUND,
AND THEN IT STOPS, AND SO DOES ITS SOUND.

WOO, WOOO!